THE TALE of LITTLE RED

Authors:
Irene Cedillo
Lourdes Martinez
Pria Zachariah

Illustrator:
Maya Pahre

For information about special discounts for bulk purchases,
please contact Tales That Tell LLC. at contact@talesthattellstories.com

ISBN: 978-1-7346386-0-8 (Hardcover)
ISBN: 978-1-7346386-1-5 (eBook)
ISBN: 978-1-7346386-2-2 (Papeback)

To our children: may you always
be dreamers, adventurous at
heart and passionate about
helping others.

Once upon a time, there was a smart and adventurous little girl.

The little girl's mother was a doctor and her father stayed home.
For the little girl's birthday, her dad made her
a beautiful red cape that she wore every single day.
Soon everyone started to call her Little Red.

One morning, Little Red's father asked her to deliver a lunch basket to her grandmother who lived on the far side of the forest.

"I filled it with fish stew, broccoli, and warm milk, her favourite foods," her father said. "Grandma is a busy scientist."

"Little Red be careful not to lose your way," said her father, "and don't stop to talk to strangers. Going through the forest can be dangerous."

Little Red put on her favorite sneakers, and hopped on her shiny scooter. She was excited. She loved visiting her grandmother's lab in the forest.

She felt safe with her many animal friends watching over her.

As Little Red approached her grandmother's lab, she became startled as a strange, furry creature with long, pointed teeth and big claws poked his head out from behind a tree. Yikes, it was a wolf! Little Red was scared!

"Hello, little girl. Where are you going?" Wolf asked. Little Red was surprised to hear the scary creature speaking in such a kind voice. He sounded almost like her mother.

Little Red remembered her father's words about strangers.
But the wolf sounded so friendly. Little Red
realized that the wolf didn't seem dangerous at all.
"I am going to my Grandmother's Lab to take her some food,"
replied Little Red. "She is a scientist and she is very busy
inventing new medicines to cure sick people."
"Ha, cures! I can get my hands on them first" thought the wolf.

"Would you like to play a game?" asked the wolf in his kindest voice.

"Yes, that sounds fun," said Little Red.

"I'll race you to your Grandmother's Lab. I'll go this way and you go that way and we shall see who arrives there first."

Little Red continued along the path as the wolf sped off through the trees. He tricked Little Red by taking a secret shortcut that quickly got him to grandmother's lab.

The wolf peeked through the window and saw Grandmother busily experimenting. Excited, he rapped on the door: KNOCK! KNOCK! Grandmother opened the door and was frightened to see the wolf.

She started to run, but the wolf was faster.
He quickly caught her and locked poor Grandmother in the closet.

"Finally!" said the cunning wolf. "Now, the cure will be mine!"

He put on one of Grandmother's white lab coats. "I look just like a scientist!!!", he exclaimed as he admired himself. Quickly, he got to work.

It was not long before
Little Red came through
the door,
singing happily, thinking
she had won the race.

"Granny! Granny!" called Little Red.
"Who's there?" said the wolf, trying his best grandmotherly voice.
"It's me, Little Red."

"Come closer, my dear. Let me see what's in the basket,"
the wolf said sweetly.

Little Red moved closer. "Grandmother looks so different!"
she thought. "Maybe she is not feeling well."

"Granny, Granny, your eyes look so big!"
"That is so I can get a better look at you," replied the wolf.

"Granny, Granny, your ears look bigger, too!"
"That's so I can hear you better," the wolf continued.

"Granny, Granny, your hands look strange too!

"They'll work just fine to grab you!" howled the wolf.

The wolf reached for Little Red, but she was furiously fast. She raced away yelling, "Help me! Help me!"

Luckily, Little Red's mother stopped by to visit Grandmother. But where was she? Little Red's mother heard Red's cries and saw her race by.

Mother caught the wolf and grabbed him by his ears. "Why are you tormenting Little Red?" she demanded. "And where is Grandmother?"

This time, it was the wolf who was scared! He was trembling as he confessed, "My brother is back at our den and is very sick. I think he has a bad case of Wolfuenza. I am just trying to find medicine to help him."

"Well, why didn't you just say so, Mr. Wolf?" asked Mother. "Come with me. I have something to show you. But first, we must free Grandmother.

"And — Mr. Smarty Pants you should try being a little nicer."
Ashamed, the wolf agreed.

"Grandmother has been working hard to find a cure for Wolfluenza," announced Little Red.

"Yes!" exclaimed Grandmother. If you had just asked, I would have gladly given you the medicine. Now let's get your brother well."

With Grandmother's guidance they mixed and measured a batch of Wolfluenza Syrup.

"Make sure it's slimy, sticky and smells like pizza," said Grandmother. "Wolves love pizza!"

That afternoon they sent the wolf home to his den
with a basket of food and his brother's cure.

"Thank you all!" the wolf exclaimed.
"One day maybe I can be a real scientist, too."

That night, safely back home, Little Red's family gathered around the fireplace. Little Red told Father about everything that had happened

"I'm glad we helped the wolf, but why were you so kind after everything he put us through?" asked Little Red.

"Little Red," her mother answered, "We must learn to forgive others and be compassionate even if they behave badly. We can teach them to be kind by being kind to them ourselves."

"Yes, my dear," said Grandmother, smiling. "Today we taught the wolf how important it is to be kind and to work as a team. And, who knows? One day Mr. Wolf may even become Scientist Wolf.

Reflection Questions

* What was Little Red's behavior like? Why?

* Have you trusted a stranger? Why?

* What would you have done if you encountered Mr. Wolf?

* How do you think Mr. Wolf felt when Little Red's mom caught him chasing Little Red?

* Can you think of a time when you felt like Mr. Wolf?

* If you were Mr. Wolf what choices would you have made instead?

* What should Grandma do with the cure for Wolfuenza?

* If you were a scientist, what would you like to discover?

* How would you help other people with your discovery?

* Grandma and Little Red helped Mr. Wolf. Can you remember a time when you helped someone? How did it make you feel?

ABOUT TALES THAT TELL

Hi there - We are Irene, Lourdes, and Pria!

Tales That Tell was born out of a desire to give our kids stories that teach them values we share: equality, empathy, and creativity. The book started as a project for our own kids and blossomed into something we hope other families will relate to and enjoy. We hope that you enjoy reading this with your little ones as much as we have enjoyed writing it with ours!

Illustrator

Maya Pahre is a 14-year-old illustrator and has been passionate about drawing since she was a little kid. She was inspired by Tell That Tell stories that are meant to empower young children to reach beyond typical gender stereotypes. The Tale of Little Red is her second book project and being an illustrator for. The Tale of Little Red has been her favorite job and an amazing experience!

CPSIA information can be obtained
at www.ICGtesting.com
Printed in the USA
BVHW021706230720
584441BV00003B/76